Benched

Cristy Watson

D1051870

Orca currents

ORCA BOOK PUBLISHERS

Library and Archives Canada Cataloguing in Publication

Watson, Cristy, 1964-
Benched / Cristy Watson.
(Orca currents)

Issued also in electronic format.
ISBN 978-1-55469-409-9 (bound).--ISBN 978-1-55469-408-2 (pbk.)

I. Title. II. Series: Orca currents
PS8645.A8625B45 2011   JC813'.6   C2010-907950-7

First published in the United States, 2011
Library of Congress Control Number: 2010941956

Summary: Cody and his friends get caught up in gang activity
when they steal a park bench.

MIX
Paper from
responsible sources
FSC
www.fsc.org   FSC™ C016245

*Orca Book Publishers is dedicated to preserving the environment and has
printed this book on paper certified by the Forest Stewardship Council.*

Orca Book Publishers gratefully acknowledges the support for its publishing
programs provided by the following agencies: the Government of Canada
through the Canada Book Fund and the Canada Council for the Arts, and
the Province of British Columbia through the BC Arts Council and
the Book Publishing Tax Credit.

Cover design by Teresa Bubela
Cover photography by Dreamstime

ORCA BOOK PUBLISHERS
PO BOX 5626, Stn. B
Victoria, BC Canada
V8R 6S4

ORCA BOOK PUBLISHERS
PO BOX 468
Custer, WA USA
98240-0468

www.orcabook.com
Printed and bound in Canada.

14 13 12 11 • 4 3 2 1

Thank you, Barb, for your friendship and support. You helped this story find its way. In memoriam (1960–2009)

Chapter One

"About time, Cody." Taz had the volume cranked on his iPod. I could hear Snow Patrol screaming out their latest tune. "Where were you?"

"You're not going to believe who I was just talking to," I said as I struggled to catch my breath.

Bowman scanned the parking lot outside our high school. "Cathy?

That grade eleven you're into?"

"You mean *Cassie*?" I asked. I don't know why Bowman had trouble with her name. "I can handle Cassie. This was… well, strange."

By then Taz was already halfway to the park, our shortcut home. He was almost six feet tall and all legs. Bowman and I had to jog to keep up with him.

"I'm listening," Bowman said.

I looked over my shoulder to make sure no one was following us, and then I lowered my voice. "So I'm leaving the school, and there's this dude leaning against the bike rack, *waiting* for me. He looked familiar, like maybe he used to hang with Dylan."

A lump the size of a grapefruit formed in my throat.

Taz interrupted, "You mean someone from Beaker's gang?"

"Yeah, but I don't know his name," I said.

"What did he want?" asked Bowman. His voice sounded tight.

I hesitated before answering. Should I tell them?

Maybe I could ignore the whole thing, like it didn't happen. But knowing Taz, he wouldn't let this go. Not until he had all the details.

As we neared the west pond, I saw two guys walking our way. I couldn't tell if they were from Beaker's gang. If they were, I wasn't ready to deal with them. Not yet. Not until we decided what to do.

"So, what's up with the dude?" Bowman asked as he bent down to tie his shoelace.

The two guys were coming straight for us. Now that they were closer, I recognized the ballcap one of them was wearing. They were definitely from Beaker's gang.

"I think…what if…," I stammered, "we get an ice cream?" I felt dumb as soon as I said it. "I'll even pay." I hoped Taz and Bowman couldn't tell my nerves were heating up.

"Did someone say Blizzard?" asked Taz. "I'm in!"

Great. That would be the end of my cash, and I'd be broke for the weekend. Again. But it would mean we'd be heading away from Beaker's brutes.

"Like you ever turn down free food," said Bowman, yanking out Taz's earbuds. Taz gave him a look, but Bowman just laughed.

The Dairy Queen was only a block from our school. As we turned around, I glanced over my shoulder. I could still see the two guys. They weren't as tall as Taz, but they were chunky like Bowman. They were way bigger than me. When they saw we'd changed our route, they did the same.

In minutes we were at the restaurant. I was about to tell Taz and Bowman that Beaker's boys were behind us, but the two guys stayed on the sidewalk instead of following us inside. The one with the blue Mohawk leaned against the window and watched us through the glass.

A cold draft rippled down my neck.

We had barely sat down when Bowman started in on me. "Are you gonna finish telling us what that guy wanted?"

"Okay." I leaned in. "So, this dude asks me if I'm Dylan Manning's brother. When I say yeah, he tells me that Beaker wants to see us—the three of us. Like he knows we hang out."

"What do you mean, he wants to *see* us?" Taz sat up and scanned the restaurant.

"I don't know exactly." I poked at my sundae with my spoon, but I didn't take a bite. "He asked if we want to earn some quick cash."

"Go on," said Taz. He looked more interested than worried.

"I think he has some kind of job for us," I said.

"So, what are we waiting for? Let's go find him," said Taz, already out of his seat.

Bowman grabbed his arm. "Hang on. We gotta figure this out. You don't mess around with these guys."

"You've got a point," I said. "So how about we just…skip it?"

The gang had been cool with my brother. That didn't mean they'd be cool with us. They didn't make a habit of hanging out with grade nines. Dylan had never wanted me around, so what did Beaker and his gang want with us?

"Yeah," said Bowman. "But we can't blow them off. They'll think we're dissing them. Besides, I *am* into earning some cash. Maybe we should check out what they want before we decide. Aren't you always saying you're broke?"

I nodded.

"Then what are we waiting for?" asked Taz.

My gut said this was a bad idea. So I don't know why I said, "The dude wants to meet at nine tonight in the park."

"Then let's make sure we're not late," said Bowman.

By the time we were ready to head home, the gang guys were gone. But I had this rumble in the pit of my stomach, and I kept looking over my shoulder as we walked through the park. A sharp bite of wind followed us.

I just wanted the meeting to be over.

Chapter Two

"C'mon guys!" Taz was half a block ahead of us. We raced to keep up.

"You think the park will burn down before we get there?" Bowman said.

We stopped at the posts that are supposed to keep cyclists out of the park. The posts are pointless. People just lift their bikes over the bars.

Adults think they have everything covered. That is so far from the truth.

Tonight is a perfect example. We all told our parents we're seeing a movie at the mall. We picked *Forbidden Kingdom* because we've already seen it. If our parents ask about the show, we can fill them in. Hanging at the park isn't a bad thing, but we didn't know what was going to happen. It seemed like a good idea to have a backup plan.

My stomach was screaming for food. I had been too nervous to eat supper.

"There they are." Taz pointed past the shrubs to the pond, where I made out several dark figures.

Bowman hesitated. "Hold up, guys. Looks like there are more of them than us."

"I figured that would happen," I said, feeling the air leave my lungs.

"Okay." Bowman leaned in. "Here's the plan. Let's tell them we'll hear them out, but we've got this big party to go to."

"Party!" interrupted Taz. "I didn't know we were going to a party. I would've showered."

"We're *not* going to a party," answered Bowman. "We're saying that so we have a reason to bail."

"Right." Taz smoothed down his black hair.

"Like you would've showered anyways," said Bowman.

We laughed. Taz threw a punch at Bowman's chest, but Bowman had him in a headlock in seconds.

"Dudes," I said. "Let's get this over with."

Beaker's gang had a reputation for rearranging faces. I just wanted to get out of there in one piece.

"Okay," continued Bowman, freeing Taz from his grasp, "so we have a party to go to. If we stick to the story, maybe they'll tell us what they want and…" His voice trailed off as we neared the gang.

The sun disappeared behind the trees.

My throat felt constricted. Even Taz slowed down.

"About time you guys showed," said Beaker as we stopped a few feet away. "We don't like waiting." The other gang members nodded. He turned to me and said, "So you're Cody Manning, Dylan's little brother?"

Before I could answer, the guy with the blue Mohawk said, "That's right." And then all cheery, like he hadn't been stalking us after school, he added, "Whaz up?"

"Nothing much," I mumbled, looking at Bowman for help. Bowman just shrugged his shoulders.

"Too bad about Dylan," said Beaker. "He was a good guy." There was a murmur of agreement from the other gang members. "That's why we called you here. We look out for family." He pointed to each of his buddies. "This is Cam, Todd, Lee and Linden."

So Todd was Mohawk-boy. He moved toward me. I backed up and nearly tripped. Bowman elbowed me. It was Bowman's idea to check out what they wanted, so I wished he'd start talking. But he just stared at them.

Then Taz jumped like something bit him. "So what are we supposed to do? This job. It earns cash, right? But we gotta get going soon. We've got plans, you know. Like this big party we're going to, right, guys?" Taz was talking faster than usual and whipping his head back and forth between us and the gang.

"Whoa. Chill, buddy." Beaker rolled his eyes at Taz, then lit a cigarette. After a couple of puffs, he said, "So we can help each other out. You do something for us, and we watch your back."

Bowman bit his lip.

What had I gotten us into?

Todd and Lee were staring us down as Beaker continued, "We have one request tonight. A *test* to see if you guys have what it takes for the *bigger* jobs."

"You mean, ones that pay?" asked Taz.

I wished he would zip it.

"We gotta know we can trust you," said Beaker. He looked at each of his buddies, and then his eyes rested on me. "We *can* trust you, right, Cody?"

"Yeah…sure."

Shouldn't it be the other way around? I wanted to know we could trust *them*. I still didn't get what this was all about.

"Cam, tell them what they need to do." Beaker leaned his arm on Cam's shoulder. As Cam talked, I noticed he was missing teeth and his nose looked like it had been broken a few times.

I rubbed my nose. What if we messed up? I didn't want to think about could happen then.

"Right, so here's the deal. All you gotta do is get rid of this park bench." He pointed to the seat beside us. "We don't care how you do it, but we want it gone by Sunday. You pass this test, and we've got something that will earn you some coin."

"I prefer bills," said Taz.

Bowman pushed him into the bushes before any of the gang members could reach him and said, "He meant…thanks for giving us a chance."

"So, we clear this bench from the park before Sunday," I said. "That's it?"

"You want *more*?" The big guy with no neck and square shoulders started toward me.

"Down, Linden," said Beaker, pulling him back. "The kid was just making sure that's all we wanted." He turned to the other three guys and whispered something. They burst out laughing. Linden joined in, even though

I'm sure he didn't know what they were talking about.

"We'll be in touch," said Beaker.

They moved down the path and in seconds were out of sight.

Chapter Three

We could barely see each other. The bench was under a fir tree, and any light from nearby houses was shrouded. Bowman grabbed one side of the bench and Taz and I grabbed the other. I counted to three and we lifted.

The bench didn't move. Because we'd used a lot of force, Taz and I fell backward.

"Jeez, I think I pulled my arm out of the socket." Taz rubbed his shoulder. "Did you guys hear something crack?"

"You'll live," said Bowman.

"I forgot all the benches are stuck in the ground. How are we going to free it?" I asked.

Pulling out his pocket flashlight, Bowman shone the beam around the bench. It was made of wood and had metal armrests. Cement strips that looked like skis ran from the front legs to the back legs. The strips were buried in the ground.

"I know," said Bowman. "See if you guys can find a rock by the pond. We can hit it against the metal legs. Maybe we can break it loose?"

"Right," I said, wandering down the hill to where Taz had already disappeared. A zigzagging rabbit nearly cut me off. I heard something that sounded like laughter to my left. I peered into the bushes but couldn't see anything.

Seconds later, Taz emerged with a grin on his face. He struggled up the grassy slope and dumped a huge rock at Bowman's feet.

"Okay, here goes," said Bowman as he banged the rock against the steel leg. It made a loud crunching noise.

"Do you really think we should be doing this?" I asked.

"Do we have a choice?" Bowman asked, looking at the spot where we'd met up with the gang. "If we do what they say, maybe they'll leave us alone."

"But not before paying us, I hope," added Taz.

Bowman bashed the leg again, and the grinding sound echoed through the park. The bench wasn't coming free, so Bowman pounded once more. A window snapped open behind us, and a gruff voice bellowed, "What's going on out there?" Then he said to someone inside his house, "Nothing but stupid teenagers."

The window slammed shut as Bowman smashed the rock down again. Sparks flew, but the leg held. Taz grabbed the rock and was about to try again when a light flickered on. It was coming from the yard where the man had yelled.

"What are you punks up to? Don't think I can't see you! I'm gonna…"

We didn't wait for him to finish. Taz dumped the rock, and we took off.

Halfway through the park, I did a face-plant on the grass, my legs sprawled out behind me. Bowman nearly landed on top of me.

"Jeez, Cody. You almost took us both out," said Bowman.

"It's not like I did it on purpose!" I sat up. "Listen…I don't hear that man coming after us, do you?"

"Naw. He was just trying to scare us," said Taz. He'd come back to where I was sprawled on the ground and extended his hand to me. As he started to pull me up, a gate creaked open behind us.

I flipped up like I was in *The Matrix* and bolted for the street.

We were halfway into the next park before we slowed down. My heart was pounding against my chest.

Bowman was doubled over, trying to catch his breath. "I think we're okay."

Jumping on the spot like a terrier, Taz said, "That was cool!"

"Yeah," agreed Bowman. "What a rush!"

At first I wasn't sure I wanted to go through with this. But now that we were out of danger, I liked the adrenaline.

Besides, if we took some old bench, who was it hurting?

Chapter Four

Saturday morning came fast. I hadn't slept much. I couldn't stop thinking about Dylan. I wondered what he would do about this job with Beaker's gang. I figured he'd go for it.

Dylan was always into something. He ragged on me all the time about learning to relax and have more fun.

"Grab life by the horns," he'd say. I never got that saying, but then, I didn't usually get Dylan.

The doorbell rang as I was pulling on my jeans. It was hard to get them on in a hurry with my legs still wet from the shower. Hopping on one foot, I fell back on my bed as Taz burst through the door.

"*Nice*," he said sarcastically. "Come on. Bowman's waiting at Tim's, and I've got a maple donut with my name on it."

"All right, already," I said, grabbing a coat. "Ever heard of knocking?"

Once we arrived at Tim Hortons, I ordered hash browns and an oj. I really wanted a breakfast sandwich, but I only had a couple of bucks. Taz picked three maple donuts and a cup of coffee—like he needed more stimulants. Bowman said he'd already eaten, but he ordered another hot chocolate while I grabbed a table.

I'd just taken a bite when Taz, his mouth full of donut, started in on me.

"Look, *lover boy*, it's your girlfriend." As he laughed, bits of donut flew from his mouth. His teeth were covered in maple icing.

"Shut it, *Stewy,*" I taunted back, knowing how much he hated his real name. He clamped his mouth shut.

I tried not to be too obvious as I looked in Cassie's direction. She was with three of her friends. I took a deep breath, and, without thinking about what I'd say or do, I found my feet taking me to the counter, where the girls were placing their orders.

"Hey, Cassie," I mumbled. I'd never stood this close to her before. She smelled like peppermint. As she turned toward me, I felt this sudden urge to check out the floor. My mouth stalled, and I had a brain freeze.

The girls were snickering, so I forced out some words. "I...needed some napkins...and...and ketchup."

Good thing I added the last part, because Cassie's friends were looking over at Taz and Bowman, and I'm sure they'd spotted the container of napkins in the middle of our table.

"Hey," Cassie smiled. "It's Cody, right? You submitted an application for the school paper?"

"Yeah. So what are you up to?" I said coolly, realizing too late she'd asked me a question.

Brianna, the tallest of her group, sneered at me. "Gee…I don't know. Getting *coffee*?" She laughed, and the other girls joined in.

Cassie didn't look at them. "Listen, come by the library third block on Monday. I can fill you in on the process. We've been going over the applications and, if I remember right, your writing is really strong. You have a good chance of getting on the paper."

I wanted to answer, but the lady behind the counter jammed several ketchup packages into my hands and waved me aside. I nodded and then slouched back to our table.

My heart was pounding faster than last night!

I was glad the girls took a table on the other side of the coffee shop where they couldn't see us. Why didn't I think about what to say before going over there? Now I'd made an idiot of myself in front of Cassie.

"Thought you said you could handle her," Bowman taunted.

Taz looked like he was about to razz me too, so I said, "Hey, shouldn't we be figuring out a plan for tonight? I mean, before it gets dark."

While Taz and Bowman talked, my mind wandered. Cassie said she thought I might be picked to write for the student newspaper. Since she was an editor, that meant I'd get to spend time with her. And I really wanted to be a journalist.

"Right, Cody?" Taz was staring me down.

"Right…what?" I said.

"Told you he wasn't listening," said Taz.

"Okay. So, tonight," said Bowman, "Taz and I were saying we should take shovels to the park to dig the bench loose."

"It'll be heavy, but we can use your sled to get it out of there," said Taz. "That was my idea. Whaddya think?"

"Sounds good!" I still had my eyes on Cassie's side of the coffee shop. "But I'll have to look for the sled—we haven't used it since we lived in the mountains. And we'd better be quiet. We don't want to wake that crazy neighbor." I slurped the last of my orange juice. "Last thing we need is the cops after us."

Bowman ran his hand over his spiked hair, and Taz whistled. They seemed pleased with themselves.

As we left the coffee shop, I glanced at Cassie. She watched as we went out the door.

Chapter Five

After supper we were back at the bench. The sky wasn't as dark as last night. A bright orange moon hovered above the rooftops of the houses beside the park. It was quiet, except for a dog barking a few yards away.

"Pass me your flashlight, Cody," said Bowman. I gave him the big flashlight we take camping. He shone the beam around the edge of the bench.

"Can anyone tell me why we didn't come here earlier, while it was still light?" I asked.

"What for?" responded Taz.

"So we could check things out. You know, make sure our plan will work."

"What? Now you don't have any faith in us?" Bowman snarled. "Seemed like a good enough plan when you were busy drooling over Cassie."

"Leave her out of this," I snapped.

I wished we'd figured out what to do with the bench once we got it on the sled. Wouldn't a good reporter think ahead?

"What's there to plan?" asked Taz. "We dig, we load, we carry. Seems simple enough to me."

"Fine." I coughed and rubbed my hands together. It was barely the end of September, but already the nights were cold.

Bowman lifted his shovel and jammed it deep into the earth.

Always on another track, Taz blurted, "I think I've got a splinter!"

"Like we're going to let you off that easy," said Bowman, now hauling dirt in a line around his side of the bench.

"Dude, this is a lot of work. Who knew this thing was buried halfway to Australia?" Taz rested his arms over his shovel. He stayed that way for several minutes while Bowman and I continued digging.

I could tell Bowman was mad. Taz was oblivious and not helping us get the bench out. After a few glares in Taz's direction, Bowman whacked the shovel out from under his resting arms.

The metal handle made a loud *CRACK* as it hit the sidewalk.

"Great, now look what you made me do," complained Taz.

"Maybe if you were *helping* instead of standing around."

Worried someone might hear, I said, "Dudes, let's just finish this!" I held my breath and waited, but it was quiet.

I pushed my shovel deep into the ground with my foot. The earth loosened.

"Hey, look," said Taz. "Cody's got it."

We began working the edges around the bench. It was almost free when suddenly a bright light was shining in my face.

"You bloody hoodlums. What did I tell you?" the man yelled from his porch. "Don't you kids ever listen?" He started toward the fence for a better view. His flashlight now beaming on the bench, he added, "And what the hell are you doing there, anyway?"

Taz raised his shovel and stood in attack mode.

I felt drops of sweat run down my neck. My mouth was dry. Hurting this old guy was not part of the plan.

"We lost something last night and came back to look for it," said Bowman, moving in front of the bench. "We didn't mean any trouble."

"Nice one," whispered Taz.

I tried to block the man's view by standing next to Bowman.

"I don't care what you're doing. The police are on their way—they'll take care of you. Ruddy punks." The man's voice trailed off as he returned to his house.

We dug faster.

I wondered if he'd really called the cops—and how long would it take them to get here?

Almost in answer to my thought, the faint sound of sirens whirred in the distance.

"Dudes, let's go!" Taz was really working now.

The sirens grew louder. If we didn't get this bench out tonight, who knows what the gang would do to us? Besides, I didn't want to let my friends down. I dug and lifted the dirt once more. Then the sirens stopped.

"Do you think they're gone?" asked Taz, looking around frantically.

"I don't know." Bowman's body was tensing up like an animal ready to fight for its kill. "Maybe they're over by the park entrance?"

"That doesn't give us much time," said Taz.

"Hey, put your shovels in beside mine," I said quietly. "I think I've got it." If we hurried, maybe we could get out of here without being caught.

My end of the bench lifted easily. In seconds we had it out of the ground and on its side. Hoisting it onto the sled, we loaded the shovels and gear onto the seat.

Each of us had a section of the rope, while Bowman counted, "One, two, three…PULL." But the sled didn't budge.

I felt rope burns on my hands. "Great! Now we're going to have to carry it."

"Maybe not," said Bowman, grabbing the sledgehammer from the rest of the gear.

"Good call bringing that along," said Taz.

Bowman hit one of the metal legs and freed it from the concrete. It made a lot of noise.

My heart went into high gear. We were so close to our goal. All I cared about now was getting out of the park with the bench. I was certain Taz and Bowman felt the same way.

Bowman whacked the other leg. It came free too. It helped that the concrete was already split on Bowman's side. The asphalt cracked, and a big chunk broke off.

"Do you hear those voices?" I whispered. They weren't close, but I could hear people talking to the right of us.

Panicking, Taz yelled, "It's the cops!" He picked up one end of the bench. I joined him, while Bowman grabbed the other side. It was still heavy, but our adrenaline must have kicked in, because we were hustling down the path and almost out of the park in seconds.

As we crossed the street, the shovels and sledgehammer went flying off the bench. The sound echoed down the road.

My heart felt like it was in my mouth.

We froze.

Everything seemed quiet.

I couldn't see anyone following us. I was about to tell the guys we were safe when a light flashed on in the nearest house.

Taz yelped. Throwing our gear onto the bench, we lifted it and bolted off the street into the next park. The sirens faded in the distance.

"Okay, we gotta find a place to dump this stupid thing," said Taz after we'd been running for several minutes. "I can't carry it another foot." The bench practically fell from my hands. Taz and Bowman put their ends down on the sidewalk.

Without planning to, we'd gone toward Bowman's house. We were only half a block away. Maybe we could stop there?

Pain was shooting down my arms.

Bowman sat on the grass under a tree. "I've got an idea," he began. "Let's lug this thing to my garage and use my dad's tools to take it apart. We can ditch the concrete in the alley and…"

"And burn the wood in your fire pit," finished Taz.

"Sounds good," I said, my breath still shallow. "Think we can do this without your folks wondering what's going on?"

"Sure. I'll say we decided to take apart an old crate we found. I'll ask my dad if we can use the wood for the fire."

"I get the sledgehammer," offered Taz. "I've got a ton of energy to burn."

"Good," I said. "Then use it to get this thing to Bowman's house." The bench seemed impossibly heavy now.

Chapter Six

I woke up with socks in my mouth. At least that was how my mouth felt after tossing and turning all night. It didn't help that I had forgotten to brush my teeth when I got home. I was in a hurry to get to bed so my mom and dad wouldn't confront me about being out so late. But they never said a word. They hadn't even said *hi* when I came in. They just stared at the TV.

Part of me wished they would get mad.

At least then I would know they remember they still have another son.

The doorbell rang. I could feel my heart punching my insides. Maybe it was the police? Or did that old guy figure out where I live?

But then my dad hollered up the stairs, "Are you awake?"

Seconds later Taz was in my room. My eyes were still glued shut with sleep, and in my rush to get dressed, I was trying to pull my pants on over my pajama bottoms.

"You wore that shirt yesterday."

"Right," I said, pulling on another shirt. "I didn't get much rest. How 'bout you?"

"Slept like a puppy." Taz grinned and tousled my hair. "Come on. Bowman's meeting us at Tim's. Wasn't that cool last night? I can't believe we didn't get caught. And how about Bowman's dad?

He didn't even ask where we got all that firewood. Know what was best?"

"Dodging the cops?" I guessed.

"Nope. Roasting marshmallows in the fire pit. I can hardly wait until May when we go camping. Man, I love marshmallows! Come on, I'm getting hungry." He took the stairs three at a time.

The kids across the street had set up hockey nets and were sticking a ball across the pavement. My next-door neighbor was washing his car.

"Hi, Cody. How are you doing?"

"Okay, Mr. Stevens."

"Off to lunch, are you?"

I looked at my watch and sighed. I'd already wasted half the day. I'd planned to look Cassie up online to see if I could learn more about my chances for the school paper. I had to make sure she'd really said that stuff about me at the coffee shop yesterday.

Would I get picked to be a reporter?

Could I spend more time with her?

All this, plus thoughts of last night, were jumbling up my brain. I had trouble focusing on Taz's words. He was in his usual mode of mouth and legs going faster than the rest of him, so I wasn't missing much.

Now that we had gotten rid of the bench, we needed to figure out what to do next. Bowman was already at Tim Hortons, sitting at a table near the back. In front of him were an empty coffee cup and a plate. He stopped strumming his fingers as we sat down.

"What took you so long? Feels like I've been here for hours. That guy over there is on his thirteenth donut."

"I had trouble getting started today," I replied, sitting across from him. "So, did your dad say anything about the firewood, or all that metal in the garage?"

"Naw. I hid that stuff up high on a shelf. My dad never looks up there. Every time Mom asks him to clean the garage, he just sweeps the floor."

We all laughed.

"When are we supposed to meet up with Beaker and those guys?" I asked, eyeing the muffins.

"Dunno. They didn't say. How 'bout we scout out the parks and hang around till we see them?" answered Bowman.

"Right," said Taz, heading toward the door. "Then let's go."

As I followed him, I realized I was starving. I wished I had cash so I could get something to eat first.

In minutes we were at the park. Geese lounged on the sidewalks and munched grass. The goslings usually tried out their wings this time of year. Several ducks were waddling down the hill toward the water, where a quiet heron was standing on one leg. Those birds ought to win

awards for patience. I never see them
move. It's like they can wait for hours
for a fish to be in the right spot.

"Hey, check out the turtle," said Taz
as he jumped the chain fence and started
after it.

"Like it stands a chance against
you." I laughed. Things felt good right
now. I wished we weren't meeting up
with the gang. Even as I thought this,
I spotted them up ahead. I grabbed
Bowman's sleeve. "There they are."

Taz stopped in his tracks and turned
to follow my pointing finger. He jumped
the fence and slipped in beside me. We
walked close together as we moved
toward the group.

The guys were wearing hoodies that
shielded their faces. But I could tell
which one was Linden by his size—he
was a good foot wider than the rest of
them. Beaker was standing nearest to us,
his arms folded across his chest.

"I'm impressed!" he said as we approached. "I didn't think you guys had it in you. But you got the job done."

"Yeah, I thought when that dude came out…"

"What Linden means," Beaker cut in, "is that he thought you were going to chicken out. But you took care of things. I like that."

So they *had been* spying on us.

Maybe they've been watching us for a while? We weren't too observant if we missed someone as big as Linden. I looked at Bowman. His eyes were narrowed like he was thinking the same thing as me.

"So, does that mean we're in?" asked Taz.

"You're at the door, that's for sure," said Beaker. "Cam. Tell them what we want them to do next."

"Okay—so, listen up." We moved into a tighter circle as Cam lowered his voice. "Here's the deal. We want you to sit at the mall and watch cars."

"Oh, like that sounds fun!" said Taz. Bowman stomped on his foot. Taz let out a yelp, but didn't say another word.

Beaker shook his head, then nodded for Cam to continue.

"So, you keep an eye out for certain vehicles. We'll give you a list with the makes and license plates of each one."

As Cam paused, Lee jumped in. "When you see one of the cars, you call this number." He handed Taz a paper.

Alarm bells were going off in my head.

"Each phone call that's good is worth twenty bucks," Beaker said while looking at Taz, who had this crazy grin on his face.

I could tell Taz was only interested in the cash. Bowman's eyes were fixed on the ground.

With a nod from Beaker, the gang closed in around us.

The only way out was to agree.

"So that's all we've got to do?" My voice sounded small, even though I was trying to appear confident. "Watch cars?"

"For now. That's our next test for you guys," said Beaker. "Are you game?"

"When do we start?" asked Bowman.

"You can start tomorrow and meet us back here with a progress report. Around eight," said Cam. Then they strolled off down the path.

I could see the headline now: *Boy, 14, Caught Red-Handed...With List.*

But that was just the beginning. Now I understood what was happening.

This test was part of an initiation.

The gang was grooming us for something bigger. Even though they were gone, I felt like they were still peering over our shoulders.

"What are we going to do now?" asked Bowman.

"Make some easy cash," answered Taz.

"You don't get it!" I kicked the ground, and a patch of grass went flying. "This isn't about money. We're already in too deep. I wish my brother never got us into this stupid mess."

Taz looked at Bowman, and then he said, "But Dylan isn't even alive. How do you figure this is his fault?"

I couldn't believe they didn't get it. I walked off without saying a word.

Chapter Seven

The next morning, I wished I hadn't stomped off. Taz got me all riled up about my brother. If Dylan were still around, he wouldn't have let the gang come after us. Would he?

And stealing a bench was one thing, but now would Beaker think he owned us?

As if worrying about that wasn't enough, I was supposed to meet Cassie today. I looked in the mirror. Even though I'd tried gel, my hair was going in every direction, like my thoughts. There's no way I'd make a good impression. I grabbed my ballcap as the doorbell rang. It was still in my hands when I ran to answer it.

"Dude, what happened to your hair?" Taz tried fixing it, but pulled his hand back, rubbing the extra gel on his pants. It left a streak down his leg.

"You're not mad about yesterday?" I asked.

"Look, I should've kept my big trap shut. I never meant anything bad about Dylan. I was just trying to figure out what our plans are with Beaker. You know we can use the cash."

I didn't want my parents to hear us, so I threw my knapsack over my shoulder and pushed Taz out the door.

I'm not sure my parents would have done anything anyway. Ever since my brother's death, they've been doing this zombie act. I missed our old family. Even though Dylan always picked on me and thought I was a pain in the butt, I missed him too.

I got Taz on a different track by talking about music, and in minutes we were at the school. Bowman was waiting outside the south doors.

"So, I was thinking," he said as we entered the building. "We should figure out what to do after school today."

"I say we go for it," said Taz as he maneuvered through groups of students. "My eagle eyes can spot anything—miles away."

"We should meet at the mall to plan our next move," said Bowman. "That way, if we're being watched, it looks like we're doing what they asked."

I was about to respond when the bell sounded. Since their first-block teacher had a habit of locking the door if you were late, Taz and Bowman took off down the hall.

I could barely concentrate through math. English was second block, and I was looking forward to seeing Ms. Cindy. Not only was she a cool teacher that let us use her first name, but she was also the sponsor teacher for the school paper. I had good grades on my writing assignments so far, and I was hoping that would help my chances with the paper.

I could tell something was wrong as soon as I walked into the room. It was dead silent, even though Ms. Cindy usually lets us talk as we settle in. She had a funny look on her face, and her eyes were puffy, like she hadn't slept.

"Cody, Melinda. Take your seats."

I slid behind my desk while Melinda grabbed a chair by the window.

Sighing, Ms. Cindy moved to the front of her desk and leaned against it. Her arms were folded across her chest.

"I'd planned to start our new novel, *Something Wicked This Way Comes*," she said. "I was going to tell you a circus came to town and you've been given free tickets to ride the carousel. Only this carousel makes you older or younger, depending on whether it goes forward or backward. Which way would you choose to ride, and why?"

A couple of hands shot into the air to answer, but Ms. Cindy waved them away.

"See, the trouble is, I'm not up for that right now."

"What's wrong, Ms. Cindy?" asked Kara.

"Something special to me was…" She paused. She began to walk slowly around the class, her purple skirt swishing as she told us about her weekend.

"My mom lives near here, in the same house we've lived in since we were kids. It backs onto a beautiful park—over that way." She pointed out the window in the direction of the ponds.

Suddenly I felt queasy. I had to listen hard to hear her words. Ms. Cindy sounded far away.

"When my father died last year, my brother and I bought a plaque and had special words engraved on it. The city of Surrey put it on a bench by the blackberry bushes. That was my dad's favorite spot."

The room felt too small, and I wished the windows were open. It seemed all the oxygen had been sucked out of the place.

"He was always in the park—reading a book, eating blackberries." Ms. Cindy smiled. "When I visit my mom, we sit on his bench and watch the wildlife.

He used to say it sounded like a symphony in the trees."

"But what happened?" asked Melinda.

"Well, yesterday Mom and I went to the park. As we came around the pond…" She looked like she was going to cry. She moved back to her desk, pulled out her chair and sat down. Glancing around the room, she rested her eyes on me.

I felt the color leave my cheeks.

"This might be a story for the paper," she said.

Like I'll make the cut now.

"Imagine how it felt," Ms. Cindy continued, "when we discovered my dad's bench was gone."

"Gone?" said Malcolm.

I raised my hand.

"Yes, Cody?"

"Can I be excused to go to the washroom?"

"Sure. It wasn't…"

I didn't wait for her to finish as I bolted for the door.

As I raced along the hall, I wondered if I could find a carousel and ride it backward to last Friday.

Chapter Eight

I paced the boy's washroom, my insides shaky. *It's not hurting anyone.* My own words went around and around in my head. Now they sounded lame. I wondered if I could hang out here for the whole block. Then I could meet up with Cassie for third...

Cassie...what'll I say to her? But she won't know what's happened, will she?

Just then two kids from grade eight walked into the bathroom. They hustled into the stalls when they saw me. I looked at my watch. Still thirty minutes left of English. I couldn't skip now. Ms. Cindy knew I was here.

My body felt heavy as I trudged back to class. The door was open. I hesitated. Leaning against a locker, I could hear their conversation. They were talking about the novel, and it sounded like Ms. Cindy was feeling better, so I slunk back to my desk.

"I'd ride the carousel forward," said Kevin. "There's this black Honda waiting for me to get behind the wheel."

"Sweet," said Prakash.

"I wouldn't ride the carousel at all."

"Why not, Sean?" asked Ms. Cindy.

"Well, I wouldn't want to be younger and have to do school all over again." A lot of kids agreed. "And I don't want all those extra responsibilities. Not yet. I'm good where I'm at."

While the class talked about what they would do, I thought about my future. Everything seemed okay with Ms. Cindy. Maybe I still had a chance to work for the school paper?

At the end of class, Ms. Cindy handed us our novels. Slipping my ballcap out of my knapsack and putting it on, I headed to the library. Then, taking a deep breath, I opened the door.

Cassie was waiting at an oval table. She had on these cool gray jeans with a pattern down the side. Her hair was pulled back from her face, making it even easier to see her hazel eyes. When she saw me and smiled, my legs stopped working. I tripped over my own feet. As I reached for the table to balance myself, my binder and novel went flying.

"That's a great book," said Cassie, as she picked up my stuff and handed it back to me. She didn't even give me a hard time about stumbling. "You'll get to see the movie too. Ms. Cindy taught us the same unit. My group made a newspaper for the project…Speaking of newspapers, how are you feeling about your chances today?"

While she talked, I watched her mouth move. She had perfect teeth, and her lips looked really soft. As she paused, I realized she was waiting for an answer. But her words hadn't registered.

"Ah…I was thinking about something else." I felt my cheeks get warm.

"Oh yeah?"

"Yeah," I said. I had no excuse handy, so I went with the truth. "I was thinking about what happened to Ms. Cindy," I said as I sat down.

Cassie pulled her chair closer. "Isn't it terrible? What kind of creeps would do something like that?"

"*Probably creeps like me.*"

"What?" Cassie asked.

I couldn't believe what I'd just said.

"Oh…I was just agreeing with you. Yeah, what creeps."

"I know. I can't imagine how Ms. Cindy must have felt. And her poor mom—it's only been a year since her husband died. When my grandma died, it was a long time before I could think about her without crying. You know what I mean?"

"Yeah," I muttered.

But I didn't know what she meant. I hadn't cried over Dylan. I remember sitting in his room after my folks told me he'd died. I remember feeling numb.

"Sorry, Cody. I wasn't thinking about your situation. You lost your brother last year, didn't you?"

I almost couldn't answer. For the first time since his death, I felt choked up. "Yeah. It's almost his birthday. Next week he would have been nineteen."

"It must be hard for you and your parents. It was a motorcycle accident, wasn't it?"

"Yeah. But it wasn't like the paper said." I was surprised all these words wanted out. "He wasn't drinking. I know Dylan drank at parties. But he *loved* that bike. He'd never risk doing anything to it."

"What happened then?"

"I don't know. Before the accident, doctors had been testing him because he'd had these weird seizures. I think that's what happened, but the newspapers made a big deal about teens and alcohol and, of course, everyone believed *their* story."

"Is that why you want to be a reporter?" Cassie asked.

"Maybe," I said. "I just want to find the truth and write about it.

"Would you have written the story about your brother differently?" asked Cassie.

"You bet. I would have checked the medical angle way more," I answered. "I would have asked a lot of questions."

"Well, part of the reason we are meeting now is so that I can see if you're passionate about being on the paper. It takes a lot of dedication. I'm glad we talked, because there is no doubt you want to do this." Cassie put her hand on my shoulder. "And Cody, I'm really sorry about your brother."

Her skin was warm and felt good. I sort of fell into her arms and let her hug me.

Tears came fast, thinking about Dylan. "I have to go," I said, pulling away and wiping my eyes with my sleeve. "Can we talk about the paper... later?"

I needed air.

"Sure. I didn't mean to upset you."

"No, you were great."

Grabbing my stuff, I ran for the door.

Once I was outside, it was easier to breathe. I found a spot under a tree and slumped down. Crumpled leaves of brown and gold rolled past me in the wind. The word *loss* seemed sharp and jabbed at my lungs.

Anger I'd felt. A lot. Especially lately.

But *loss*, this was new, and it sat heavy on my chest.

Lunch was almost over, and I knew I had to get it together before my afternoon classes. I stood up and stretched, then headed into the school to my locker. I was about to grab an apple from my lunch bag, when Taz slammed the door shut.

"Hey, you nearly chopped my fingers in half. What gives?" I asked.

"Sorry, dude. So where the *bleep* were you at lunch?" The principal was headed our way.

"I had some stuff on my mind. Lots of homework and…"

"And a blond-haired, brown-eyed…"

"Well…yeah," I said. A thought came to me." Hey, listen. I have to get to class, but I wanted to ask you something *really* important."

Taz was down the hall and out of sight before I could continue.

Chapter Nine

The afternoon went by in a blur. I don't remember what happened in any of my classes. As I was cleaning up at the end of the day, I heard my name announced over the PA system.

"Cody Manning and Pam Swanson to the library."

I felt my heart rev up again.

They caught us?

No, they called a girl's name too. And you don't go to the library when you get in trouble.

Maybe I got the position on the paper?

I rushed to my locker, grabbed my homework and headed to the library.

Cassie and a few other students from grade eleven and twelve were already there.

"Good, now that we're together," began Ms. Cindy as Pam entered from the other door. "We have great news for both of you."

While Ms. Cindy shared that we'd be joining the newspaper club, all I could think about was her dad's bench. This should have been the happiest day of my life—but instead I felt like crap.

I mumbled "Thank you," and excused myself, saying I had a ton of homework.

Cassie followed me to the door of the library.

"Are you okay? You don't seem super happy about the news."

"No. It's not that. I'm really stoked about getting on the paper. I just…"

"You're thinking about Dylan, right?"

"Can you tell Ms. Cindy I'm sorry I have to go?"

"No problem. Here." She tore a piece of paper out of her binder and scribbled on it. "It's my phone number. Call if you need to talk."

Taz and Bowman were waiting for me on the north side of the shopping mall. The air felt crisp, like winter was coming. Taz was lying on the grass, munching on a burger and fries. Bowman was sitting up, his eyes on the parking lot.

"So where have you been?" asked Taz. "We heard your name called on the PA. What's up?"

"Nothing." I sat down between them. "It was about the school paper."

Bowman's eyes were on the cars. "Did you get it?"

"Yeah."

"Sweet. Now you'll see Miss Whatever-her-name-is every day." Taz slurped the last of his root beer through the straw. "You aren't going to stop hanging with us, are you?"

"I'm on the paper. But now I don't know. Maybe it's not what I want, after all."

Bowman and Taz exchanged glances as I picked up Bowman's burger and took three bites without even chewing. I washed them down with a swig of his root beer and let out a huge burp.

"Listen, I've got something to ask you," I said.

"Yeah?" said Bowman, grabbing his burger back. "Well, it will have to wait. Right now, we've got to figure out what to do with this stupid *list* and Beaker's gang."

"I still say we go for it," said Taz. "We need the cash, we need the fame, and we definitely need some fun."

"Pulling the prank was okay," added Bowman. "But this car stuff. You know what it will lead to."

"Yeah, twenty bucks a shot," said Taz.

"The cash isn't worth it," I said. "This is challenge number two, then what? They'll keep upping the ante, and before we know it, we've crossed a line."

Like the bench. Only Taz and Bowman didn't know yet that it belonged to one of our teachers.

"Okay, so we don't follow their instructions," said Taz, pulling out the list. "Then what do we tell them tonight at eight?"

"I don't know," I answered.

"What *do* you know?" Taz sounded rattled.

"I know I didn't go looking for them. They approached *me*, remember?" I felt my pulse quicken. "Besides, even though my brother was usually a jerk, maybe I wanted…I don't know—they all hung out. I thought maybe I'd feel…closer to him."

The guys gave me a strange look, then turned to each other. I lowered my head. "I know. It was stupid. And now this mess is all my fault."

"That's not what I was thinking, dude," said Bowman. Then he grinned. "And like you took the bench out all by yourself."

"Yeah," said Taz. "Without all my hard work, you guys would still be digging."

As we laughed, I felt my shoulders relax. A little. We weren't any closer to figuring out how to get out of this, but at least we were working together.

Halfway through the park as we headed home for supper, I realized this was a dumb move. If we wanted to avoid the gang, we should have stuck to the main streets.

Linden, Todd and some other bruiser we hadn't seen before were straight ahead of us.

Chapter Ten

I ducked behind a blackberry bush, and Bowman pulled Taz down with him so we wouldn't be spotted. Todd had his back toward us, and Linden was leaning against a birch tree. The third guy looked like a wrestler. They were talking over top of each other, like they were arguing about something.

If we turned back the way we came, we could get out of the park without them seeing us. But even as I formed this thought, Linden stood up and lumbered our way. He was cursing over his shoulder at Todd. The guy that looked like a wrestler followed Linden. They were only a few feet away.

They stopped in front of our hiding place. Linden spat into the bushes, and it splattered onto my cheek. I was about to say something when Bowman put his hand on my shoulder. He nodded for me to keep quiet. Taz was trying to stay put, even though he looked like he was ready to run.

"Can you believe that guy? Who does he think he is—the boss, or something?" yelled Linden.

"You gotta cool it, bro," said the wrestler. "You know what happened last time you crossed Beaker. Todd's not worth it."

Linden punched the air. "But he thinks he can tell me what to do. I only listen to Beaker. Not him." He staggered toward the path.

Two boys from our school were passing by. They were grade eights, but looked like they were in elementary school. Before any of us could move, Linden picked one of the boys up by the back of his shirt and threw him to the ground.

"Let's go," said Linden's friend, grabbing him by the shoulder. But Linden was kicking the boy, who had curled up in a ball. The kid's friend was looking around frantically.

I wanted to help them. I wanted Linden to stop. But what if he turned his anger toward us? I heard rustling behind me and realized Taz was backing up, still bent over so he couldn't be seen. Bowman took three steps backward.

A tree branch snapped under his feet.

Taz and I both jumped and ran. Bowman must have followed us, because I could hear him hollering, "Go!"

We ran without looking back. Soon we were near the street. I chanced a look over my shoulder. The wrestler dude was hurtling down the path.

"Don't stop!" I yelled to Taz and Bowman.

As I ran out into the street, I heard the screech of tires and what sounded like a fist punching the hood of a car. A silver Honda had almost clipped Bowman, but it served as a block between the thug and us. We kept running until we were through the second park.

I was sure my chest was going to explode, my breath was coming so fast.

"I hope those kids are okay," said Taz, checking behind him.

"We should have helped them," I said.

"I know. I wanted to. But Linden's been waiting for a chance to go after us," said Bowman. "We might have helped the kid, but then we would have been the next victims." We kept a jogging pace toward Bowman's house. Once there, we caught our breath.

From the safety of his garage, we watched the street for Linden and the other guy.

"At least we made them chase us," I said. "So they probably left the kids alone, right?"

"Yeah. I'm sure they got away. And I'm glad *we* got away," added Bowman.

"I feel like I could eat a whole cow," said Taz, hopping onto the workbench. "All this excitement makes me hungry."

"I can cook hot dogs," said Bowman, shaking his head.

"Sounds good," answered Taz.

"I don't know where you put all this food," I added, thinking about the meal he'd scarfed down at the mall.

"Right here." He smiled and pointed to his head. Bowman and I laughed.

"Hey, guys, before we eat, I have something really important to ask you."

"So ask," said Bowman. He and Taz stared at me.

I felt a lump form in my throat. "I was wondering. What did we do with all that scrap metal from the bench?"

"It's right here," answered Taz. "Don't you remember?"

"Oh, yeah. Right." I laughed. "Did you keep the plaque?"

"The plaque?" asked Bowman. "Getting sentimental, are we?"

"Naw, I was just curious." I wasn't even sure why I needed the plaque. But it had been on my mind. "So, was there, like, a lot of scrap metal?"

"Yeah," said Bowman. He pushed a stepladder over to the south wall of the garage and climbed the steps. "See." He pulled out pieces of metal from under an orange tarp. The plaque fell to the ground at my feet.

"You think you can make something outta this old junk?" asked Taz.

"Dunno. Maybe…" I picked up a metal rod and the plaque at the same time. I stuffed the plaque into my coat pocket while Taz and Bowman looked over the other pieces. "Well, we probably should get cooking before it's time for dinner," I said.

"Right," said Bowman, jamming the stuff back on the shelf.

We hung out at Bowman's until suppertime and decided to get together before eight. We needed to figure out how to handle the meeting with Beaker. After seeing Linden in action, none of us were too keen on telling the gang we wanted out.

I thought about all of this on my way home and forgot to stay on the street. I turned into the park, like always. Luckily, no one was around.

Benched

As I passed the gaping hole where the bench used to be, I shook my head. There must be at least ten benches in the park.

Why did we have to steal *this* one?

Chapter Eleven

Before supper, I went to my room to see if I could think of a way out of this job with the gang.

I passed the living room on my way upstairs. My mom was still in her housecoat, and my dad was going over bills at his desk. I took the stairs two at a time and stood outside Dylan's room.

I pulled the plaque from my pocket. It was made of brass and had old-fashioned lettering. It said: *"Beauty is truth, truth beauty...All you need to know."* Your *loving family*. Why do people always put weird sayings on these things? And what does it even mean?

Still holding the plaque, I headed into Dylan's room and sat on the edge of his bed. My mom and dad had left his room the way it was the day he died. I hadn't been in here since then. The room creeped me out before. But tonight it felt different. I looked at the picture on his wall. It was of Dylan and my dad fishing. Dylan was holding a huge salmon. The grin on my dad's face made me smile.

Instead of remembering how Dylan always yelled at me and treated me like a kid, I had a flood of good memories. Like the time he took me fishing when we were camping at Adams Lake.

He was really patient with me. We talked for hours, and he taught me how to tie a lure on my hook. When I finally snagged a rainbow trout, he helped me reel it in. It was so gross. The hook was pierced through its eye. Dylan laughed all night, retelling the story.

I picked up the model Lamborghini from his shelf and turned it in my hands. I remembered the Christmas he got it as a gift. Dylan was always up at the crack of dawn Christmas morning. He'd haul me out of bed to see our presents, his face lit up with a huge grin. The year I got the Hot Wheels racetrack, he helped me put it together and we raced my new cars all morning. He taught me how to repair a flat tire on my bike, and once he even took me on his motorcycle. Maybe he would have taken me more times if…

My eyes welled up. Jeez, ever since Cassie talked about him…

Cassie…

Ms. Cindy…

I ran my sleeve across my eyes and forced my mind back to the present. I had to figure out how to fix things so I could be on the school newspaper. Even though I didn't want to, I was going to have to talk to Ms. Cindy.

Maybe she'd forgive me if I gave the plaque back?

Who was I kidding?

Gee, Ms. Cindy, I totally trashed your dad's bench, but I managed to salvage the plaque. Where would you like it?

Now I sounded like Taz.

I grabbed a photo album from Dylan's bookshelf and headed back to my room. I opened a bag of chips and grabbed a handful as I lay on my bed and rifled through the pictures.

My eyes stopped on a photo of Dylan and me in Stanley Park. We were smiling while standing on a bench beside a cedar tree. Somebody had tagged the bench. I'd never noticed before how so many benches had graffiti all over the wood. Some even had marks on the plaques. At least Ms. Cindy's was clean. She wouldn't even need a new one if...

Suddenly, I sat up and grinned. I knew how to solve the bench dilemma!

I could look up the address for Ms. Cindy's mom, then leave the plaque in her mailbox. I bet the city replaces benches all the time. The plaque could be put on a new bench, and everyone would be happy.

The best part of this plan was that I wouldn't have to tell anyone I was involved. I could still be on the paper, I could hang with Cassie, and I didn't have to let Taz and Bowman down. It was brilliant!

I turned on my computer. While I waited for it to load my home page, I checked the time.

7:45.

I had five minutes to find her address, and then I needed to get to Bowman's house.

Chapter Twelve

Taz and Bowman were kicking a hacky sack back and forth in the driveway.

"So," I started as the hacky sack came my way. I passed it back with the heel of my foot. "What do we do about Beaker?"

"I think we have to avoid the gang. None of them go to our school," said Bowman. "So at least we're safe during the day."

"And what about after school?" asked Taz. He hit the hacky sack with his elbow to keep it in the air.

"No more shortcuts through the park, that's for sure," I said. "Maybe we could catch a ride with someone?" I instantly thought of Cassie. She had a car.

"But how long will we have to hide from them?" asked Taz. He missed the pass from Bowman and bent down to pick up the hacky sack. "I don't like the thought of someone else running my life."

"Maybe we should confront them," I said. "Tell them we appreciate their offer, but—"

Bowman cut me off. "We have better things to do?" He smirked. "Do you really think that will work?"

"Hey, I'm just trying to help." Ever since this gang thing started, we were arguing more.

Taz strolled down the driveway. "Well, whatever we decide, we better do it soon. It's eight o'clock."

"They probably don't know where we live," I said. "Yet. So maybe we should stay away tonight and hope that we think of something by tomorrow?"

"I'm game for living one more day," said Bowman.

"But we'd better think of something soon," added Taz. "They won't leave us alone for long."

We agreed to wait another day before confronting the gang. I think we were all afraid of what might happen. Stalling seemed like the best plan for now.

Taz and Bowman were more relaxed after our decision and decided they wanted to catch a movie. I was still thinking about Ms. Cindy's mom, so I opted out. I debated telling them about Ms. Cindy's dad, but I worried they'd try to talk me out of giving back the plaque. So I told them I'd catch them in the morning.

I headed to the coffee shop to wait until it got dark. When I entered the park, I kept an eye out for Beaker and the gang. Some older kids from school were hanging out near the east pond. They were laughing and drinking from a bottle they had stashed inside a paper bag. I waited for them to leave before I ventured onto the path.

Pulling out the address, I scanned the houses to see where Cindy's mom's house would be. It was easy to find the house once I got onto the street. Except for one light in the living room, the place was in total darkness. The drapes were closed and I could hear the TV. Old people always have the thing blaring. And they give *us* flack about *our* music!

As I stepped closer to the porch, I wished Taz and Bowman were with me. Maybe I should have told them, after all.

The mailbox was only a few feet away. It would take only a second to run up the stairs and drop the plaque in. But my feet felt like they were glued to the spot.

I climbed the first step. A couple walking their dog passed the house, and I found the courage to take the next step. As soon as my foot landed, the porch light came on. I missed my footing altogether and fell into a shrub.

Realizing it was only a motion sensor, I brushed off the twigs and clambered up the stairs again. The mailbox creaked like a coffin in a horror film. My hand felt jittery. I was about to drop the plaque into the mailbox when the living-room curtain moved.

I didn't wait to find out if Ms. Cindy's mom had spotted me. I bolted for the back of the house. Something brushed past my leg, and my body went into high gear.

I tore down the path. After several minutes, I looked to see if I was being followed. No one was behind me. As I turned back to face the path, I bumped into Beaker. Full-body contact.

"Sorry, I didn't mean to…I didn't see you there," I stammered and backed up.

"What are you running from? The cops?"

"No, I just…"

"Something has you spooked," he said as he moved closer. "And where were you and your buddies tonight? We waited for a half hour." He put his hand on my shoulder.

I looked to my left and then my right. There was no access to the yards. If I turned and ran back the way I came, I could run into the street and at least there would be cars around. It was so dark in the park, no one would see me. No one would know that I was about to be pulverized to mush.

I slowly backed up, knowing I'd have to time this right, because Beaker was lean and muscular. He'd be faster than me.

"Hey, you don't have to run." Beaker turned his hands up, showing me they were empty. "I'm here by myself. Sometimes I stay in the park all night. It's a good place to think."

I looked around again, trying to see behind the bushes, in case he was lying and Linden was waiting for me. But I couldn't see anyone. I still felt anxious and decided I'd better stay alert.

"So how come you didn't show up tonight?" he asked again.

"Well, we...I mean, I..." I didn't know what to say.

Beaker didn't seem as big and menacing without his gang. Maybe I could tell him? "You see, this bench thing turned out to be more than we bargained for, and I'm probably going to lose out on something I really wanted because of it. If we do more, we're going to get in trouble for sure." Even as I said it, I knew it was lame.

"I told you we'll look out for you. You're Dylan's brother." He shifted his weight. The glow from the moon shone on his face. His eyes were droopy, like he hadn't slept in weeks. With the way my house had been since Dylan died, I could understand why someone might spend all night in a park.

At least you expect the trees to ignore you.

"Look," I started. "It's not like we don't appreciate you giving us this opportunity. It's just...I'm not sure it's what we want." I was looking at the ground as I talked. As I glanced up, Beaker was nodding. "I mean, maybe another time. Just not right now."

"Kid, Dylan did something for me that the other dudes don't know about.

I wouldn't be here right now, if it weren't for him. So I can cut you some slack." He grinned. "For now."

I didn't know what to say. Was he really going to let us off that easy? If the rest of the gang were here, would he let us off the hook?

I didn't think so.

"You'd better take the offer now," Beaker added, as if he could read my thoughts. "It has a time limit, you know."

"Right," I said.

"Don't say anything to your buddies. This is between us, at least until I talk to my guys." Then he pushed past me and disappeared into the darkness.

It was late when I got home, but I slept soundly knowing that the gang would leave us alone.

For now.

Chapter Thirteen

During homeroom, Mr. Daniels told me I was supposed to meet Cassie in the library at lunch. A bunch of guys whistled and laughed. I felt my cheeks get hot.

At noon I went to the library with my lunch bag and got reamed out by Mrs. Crouch, the librarian. We all called her "Mrs. Grouch" behind her back, except once when Taz accidentally said it to her face. He got detention for a week.

Cassie was sitting by a window, reading. My stomach grumbled as I approached her table.

"Hey, Cody. I'm glad we could meet today." Gold earrings bounced as she flicked her hair. "And I'm happy you're a part of the newspaper club."

I smiled and sat down.

She moved closer to me.

"So I have your assignment. Ms. Cindy thought you and Pam could each write one article for the first edition of the school year." This time she was wearing perfume that smelled like chocolate.

"She also mentioned that, since you're in her class, she wants *you* to write the story about her dad's bench." Her eyes lit up. "Wouldn't it be cool if you discovered who stole it?"

"Right," I spluttered. I couldn't look at her. All I could think was, How cool is it to solve a crime you committed?

Out loud I said, "Sure. I hope I can figure out what happened." My throat pinched as I lied.

"Yeah. And something should be done to the idiots who took the bench." Cassie went on talking about layout, how long the article should be and how to set up the formatting.

Part of me was listening, while part of me was stuck on what she'd said. What if the *real* story ever got out? I wondered if it would make a difference if I told her that I planned to return the plaque to Ms. Cindy's mom? Would she still think I'm a jerk?

"How does that sound?" Cassie was smiling at me, waiting for my answer.

"What?" I felt my neck warm up. "Ah, right. Should I interview Ms. Cindy tomorrow during my English class?"

"Sure," she answered. "The deadline is next Monday. I'm sure your story will be great." She waved at Brianna, who had just entered the library. That was my cue to leave.

"Thanks, Cassie." I darted from the table before Brianna could join us.

How could I interview Ms. Cindy without giving away our part in this?

My insides felt all twisted up as I headed outside to find Bowman and Taz. I wolfed down my lunch, since there wasn't much time before the bell would go.

"Dude, we're over here." Taz was leaning against a bike rack, playing with the gears on some guy's BMX.

Bowman pushed Taz's hands away from the bike. "So, what's our plan for after school? Do we meet up with Beaker?"

"Yeah," answered Taz. "I couldn't stop thinking about that kid Linden bullied. I don't want to be next on his hit list."

"What do you think, Cody?" Bowman was eyeing a girl in grade twelve.

"I dunno," I said. My lungs felt squished as I thought about last night. I hoped that Beaker had told his goons we were finished. What if Linden didn't care?

"Maybe we could meet up with them and say we didn't see any of the cars?" said Taz.

"Yeah, but then they'll expect us to stick to the deal," I said, trying to buy time to think. I was getting a headache.

"Hey, Taz. Where is the list, anyway?" asked Bowman, tapping his spiked hair.

"That's the ticket!" Taz crossed his feet and spun around, like he was doing a hip-hop move. "I lost the list. I mean, for real. When we were at the mall last time. When I got home, it wasn't in any of my pockets. I've been trying to figure out how to tell you. Now it may be the best thing that happened." He had a goofy grin on his face.

"So, we tell Beaker we lost the list," said Bowman. "He'll give us a new one, and then we have a couple of days to make a better plan."

I looked at Bowman and Taz. The idea made sense. Since I had a bigger problem to deal with at the moment, I said I'd go along with them.

Chapter Fourteen

On my way to English, I decided to make a list of questions to ask Ms. Cindy so that I wouldn't mess up and let on that I'd stolen her dad's bench. If I made them tonight, I could interview her tomorrow morning—after a good night's sleep. I wished I didn't have her class today. Then I wouldn't have to see her until I had everything sorted out.

When I arrived, Ms. Cindy was handing out projects for the novel. As I passed her on the way to my seat, she turned to me and said, "Perfect timing. We can do the interview right now."

My heart revved up. I wasn't ready.

"How about we sit by my desk, Cody? That way I'm available if there are questions on the project."

I felt sweat pool under my arms. "Ah...sure."

I took out some paper and grabbed my pen from my desk. My classmates were busy working.

I had to think like a reporter. What do they usually ask first?

"So, what's your dad's name? I mean, what *was* your dad's name?" I was screwing up already.

"Scott. But you should use Mr. Connelly for the paper."

"Can you tell me what happened on the weekend?" I looked at my hands.

They were shaking. I tried to think ahead to what I should ask next while Ms. Cindy shared the story of how the bench was taken.

"Aren't you going to write this down?" she asked.

"Oh, yeah…well, I remember this part from class the other day." Barely recovering, I added, "And, what effect has this had on you and your family?"

"Well, for starters, my mom hasn't slept for days. Just like when my dad first passed away. And she isn't eating. I guess it's like losing him all over again."

My shirt tightened around my neck, and I had trouble swallowing. I decided taking notes might be a good idea. That way, I wouldn't see Ms. Cindy's face.

She continued, "I'm frustrated this happened. You see, for us that bench was my father and his memories wrapped up in one."

"But, isn't it…too painful to remember?" I asked.

"Sometimes. But the bench was the keeper of *good* memories."

She cleared her throat, and finally I looked up. Her cheeks were flushed and her eyes were watery. I felt like a total loser.

"Why don't you replace the bench?" I figured if I asked another question, I could keep my heart from pounding in my head.

Could someone my age die of a heart attack? It sure was working overtime this week!

"I don't know, Cody. Replacing a bench is a lot of work." She looked around the room, checking if any students needed help. "I know you understand. Cassie told me you've been thinking about your brother lately." She put her hand on mine. "How are *you* doing?"

Great. Not only was I a jerk for what I did to Ms. Cindy and her family, now she was concerned about my feelings. I didn't know what to say.

"It must be hard for you and your folks. I had a lot of years with my dad. I can't imagine what your parents must feel, losing their son so young."

I looked out the window. The oak tree barely had any leaves left on its branches.

I tried to catch my breath and croaked, "Is it okay if we just stick to the interview?"

"Sure, Cody. I didn't mean to pry."

I managed to ask a few more questions, and then Sean and Melinda interrupted with stuff about their projects. I had enough to start the article, and I told Ms. Cindy I'd check back with her if I needed more.

The last half of class dragged on forever. Ms. Cindy's words kept replaying in my head. Even though my eyes were on my paper, I couldn't make sense of what I was reading. I didn't even begin my project.

The rest of the afternoon went by just as slowly.

I didn't care now if somebody knew what we'd done. I deserved to get caught and be dropped from the paper.

We took the long way home after school. Bowman and Taz were still trying to figure out what to do about Beaker and his gang. They weren't as sure now as they had been earlier that saying we lost the list was going to work. They were tossing ideas around and asking for my input every three seconds, while Taz surfed on his iPhone.

My headache was turning into a migraine. My mom had been having a lot of migraines since Dylan's death. Now I understood how she felt.

The pain was brutal.

"Oh my god! Look at this," said Taz, flipping his phone in our direction. He had his Facebook page up, and under the school group there was a message about the bench.

It was posted with a profile name I didn't recognize, but the person wrote: *My house backs onto the pond. I saw what happened from my bedroom window, and I know the bench stealers attend our school.*

I bit my lip as I talked. "Do you think they know it was us?" The metallic taste of blood filled my mouth.

"It was dark, dude. Maybe they only saw shadows?" answered Taz.

"Maybe this is the break we've been looking for," said Bowman. "I think I know how we can get out of this mess with the gang."

"What are you thinking?" I asked.

"We tell the truth. Somebody saw us do the bench job, and they likely spotted us with the gang too," he looked relieved. "Those guys aren't going to want to risk an association if they think someone will tell the cops."

Bowman was right. And this way, Beaker wouldn't think I snitched to my friends. So that meant we'd probably be cool with the gang.

But someone spotting us meant I had to fix the bench problem with Ms. Cindy. Now.

Chapter Fifteen

My mom was sitting on the couch staring off into space as I entered the house. I wanted to tell her what was happening, but I didn't know where to start. Going toward the kitchen to make a snack, I turned at the doorway. My shoulder brushed against the calendar.

"Mom. Did you know it's almost Dylan's birthday?" I asked.

My mom didn't look up and didn't answer. She seemed so small, sitting there on the couch. I thought about what Ms. Cindy said—how my parents had such a short time with Dylan. I went and sat beside her and put my hand on her lap. She took my hand in hers. Her fingers were cold.

"How about I make us dinner?" I asked. She looked at me like she was seeing me for the first time.

"You're a good son, Cody," she said before staring at the wall again.

Maybe she was watching a silent movie of the past, when we were all a family.

I had to do something. All this stress was weighing me down. I had to make things better.

Before starting dinner, I went online to find the phone number for Parks and Recreation. It took some time to figure out who I needed to talk to, but the lady that answered the phone was really patient. After what seemed like years, some guy finally came on the line.

"Can I help you?" he asked.

I felt calm for the first time since this whole mess started. "Yeah. Can you tell me how I get a bench replaced in the park?"

"Sure, which park are you looking for?"

I explained the details, leaving out the part about *how* the bench went missing. I also asked if I could get an inscription added.

"Well, that will cost you," he said.

I hadn't counted on a cost. The price was steep. Good thing I already had the plaque. That meant I wouldn't have to pay *as* much. I had a savings bond from my great aunt. I hoped I'd be able to use that. In the meantime, I'd have to ask for an advance on my allowance. Like three years' worth!

All I had to do now was meet a city worker in the park with the plaque and he'd secure it to the bench. We agreed to meet on Saturday afternoon.

As usual, Mom and Dad were quiet during dinner. Instead of being silent too, I decided to jump in and start a conversation.

"I got picked to be on the school paper," I said.

But I'll be kicked off tomorrow when I tell the teacher what I did to her dad's bench.

"That's great, Cody," said my dad. "Is this for one of your classes?"

"Naw, it's after classes."

"You can stay caught up in your schoolwork if you do this too?" Mom asked.

Dad and I looked at her at the same time. My dad smiled and put his hand over hers. The rest of the meal was quiet, but I felt hopeful for the first time in months.

I couldn't sleep most of the night. I worried about how I was going to tell the guys my plan. What would they think if they knew I interviewed Ms. Cindy about the bench? And then there was the problem with the message on Facebook.

When I finally slept, my dreams were filled with images of the park. Every house had windows that looked like giant eyes watching my every move. I woke up feeling like I hadn't rested at all.

While eating breakfast, I decided not to tell Taz and Bowman what I was up to. At least, not until after I'd met with Ms. Cindy. Instead of waiting for them, I went straight to Ms. Cindy's room before the first bell.

She was sitting at her desk, marking papers. As I approached, she smiled. "Hi, Cody. You're here early. Do you have more questions for me?"

"No. Well, sort of." My mouth felt dry again.

Even though this was the right thing to do, it was a lot harder than lying. Part of me felt like bolting. I hadn't said anything incriminating yet, so maybe...

"I can answer anything you'd like."

"Well," I started.

The story spilled out. I told her it was a dumb prank some older kids dared me to do. That part was honest. "I guess I wanted to be cool. I didn't think it would hurt anybody. I definitely didn't think about the bench *belonging* to someone."

Ms. Cindy shook her head. "You know how much this hurt my family, Cody. I wish you'd thought about the consequences before—"

"I know," I interrupted. "I shouldn't have taken the bench. And most of all, I should have owned up to it right away. Now I've made things worse."

"Well." Ms. Cindy sighed. "I'm glad you told me what happened. It takes courage to come clean."

She moved from her chair to lean against the desk so we were almost at eye level with each other. "It must have been hard for you to do the article on me. That was pretty gutsy."

"You mean, pretty stupid. Only an idiot would try to cover up like that. You'll never trust me again. I totally understand why you'd kick me off the paper." I turned to leave the class.

Ms. Cindy sighed again. "Cody, I'm not that kind of person. I don't hold grudges, and I meant it when I said it takes courage to come forward. I *would* still like you to be on the paper. I think you show great potential in your writing." She put her hand on my shoulder. "I only wish there were some way to fix things."

I couldn't believe it! I figured that was it—I'd blown everything.

This wasn't as bad as I thought it would be, and I hadn't even told her the best part yet.

"Are you free on Saturday?" I asked.

"Changing the subject, are we?"

"Well…yeah. I need you and your mom to come to the park. You can invite your brother too, if you want."

Ms. Cindy's shoulders relaxed. "Cody Manning, what do you have planned?"

Chapter Sixteen

I met up with Taz and Bowman in the hall between our first two periods.

Taz made a beeline for me. "Dude, someone from your English class said you were interviewing your teacher yesterday." He looked at me accusingly. "They said it had something to do with the stolen bench."

"I was going to tell you. I thought I had one more day. But things didn't work out the way I planned."

"So, what did you say about us?" Taz kicked the locker next to him.

"I didn't say anything about you guys. Honest. I only asked questions about Ms. Cindy." I looked around to make sure no one could hear us. "Even if I added something about who did it, I'd keep you guys out."

"But you *aren't* going add anything, are you?" asked Bowman.

"I don't know," I said. "I still have to finish the article, and I have a science test tomorrow." With all the events of this week, I hadn't even studied.

"You'd better keep us out of this," said Taz as he stormed off. Bowman shrugged his shoulders and followed Taz.

"But, guys," I said to the empty hall.

I knew they'd be upset. Now I could only hope that once they had a chance to cool off, they'd understand.

I figured since I'd messed up with Taz and Bowman, I might as well fess up with Cassie too. She was in the cafeteria at lunch.

"Hi, Cody," she said as I approached her table. "How'd the interview go?"

"Well," I said. It was harder telling her than Taz and Bowman. "I...I kind of left out some details when we talked about the bench before."

She looked at me. "What do you mean?"

"We, I mean," I stammered, "*I*...was responsible. *I* stole the bench."

She stood up so fast she practically knocked her juice into my lap.

"I have to talk to Ms. Cindy," she said. "I can't let this go, Cody."

"No, it's okay. I mean...I already told Ms. Cindy. I'm going to fix it."

"How could you do this? And I thought you really wanted to be a reporter."

She stormed off before I could say, "But I do want to be a reporter."

I was disappointed, but figured since I was still on the paper, we'd get to spend time together and she'd get to know me better. *The real me*. Then, who knows?

I made dinner the next two nights and helped my dad clean up the dishes. We were all talking more at the dinner table, and my mom even put on a dress before coming down for supper Friday night.

On Saturday, I met Ms. Cindy and her family in the park. Some guy from the city was there in his coveralls, putting in the bench. Ms. Cindy's mom looked frail. I was learning that losing someone special could do that to people.

"Hi, Cody," chirped Ms. Cindy. "I'd like you to meet my mom, Mrs. Connelly. And this is my brother, Clyde."

"Pleased to meet you," they answered together.

I'm not so sure I'd be pleased to meet the person who'd vandalized *my* property, but they seemed like a forgiving family.

The guy from the city turned to me when he finished securing the bench. By then, a small crowd of people had gathered to see what was happening. Most of them were seniors who lived in the area.

"Do you have the plaque?" he asked.

I pulled it from my pocket and handed it to him. Mrs. Connelly looked a little surprised. Then Ms. Cindy came over and handed the city worker something. He smiled.

After a few minutes the plaque was in place. I moved forward to check it out.

"Hey, that's not the one I gave you," I said.

Ms. Cindy smiled and put her hand on my shoulder. I leaned in closer to read the inscription.

It read: *To our loving father and husband. Your symphony plays on.*

The next line got me choked up. *And we honor Cody Manning's memory of his brother, Dylan.*

For the second time in days, I had to fight back tears. I hugged Ms. Cindy and thanked her.

"I hope your family is okay with us recognizing Dylan this way."

"It's perfect," I said. The sun glinted off the plaque. "But how did you know?"

"I didn't. Well, not until you invited us here." Ms Cindy put her arm through her mom's. "I thought about what you said when we did the interview. You asked why I didn't replace the bench. It dawned on me then that this would be a good way for my family to move forward, to get past this. And then

I wondered if that's what you were doing. Making amends."

I looked out at the pond. I'd fixed things with Ms. Cindy. And even though Taz and Bowman had been giving me the silent treatment, maybe things would be okay with them too.

Since I was still on the paper, I decided to write about what really happened—keeping Taz and Bowman out of the story, of course. As for the gang, we'd probably have to lay low for a while.

After saying goodbye, I watched Ms. Cindy and her family leave the park. Their arms were intertwined. I felt an ache in my belly.

Maybe I could bring my mom to the park tomorrow. Maybe we could sit on the bench and look at the ducks. Maybe we could eat blackberries together.

Acknowledgments

Thanks to my keen teens: Zak, James and Sean; and my writers' group: Barb, Lois, Mary, Michele, Sushill, Marcella, and Wendy and Shar. Special thanks to my family: Mom, Dad and Lise; to Judy and to my best friend, Lynne. I also want to thank Melanie, my editor, for helping me make my first novel a better story.

Cristy Watson is a teacher who loves reading and writing poetry and YA novels. She hosts open-mic readings at her local coffee shop, and she likes to enter writing contests, especially ones where there is a challenging time limit. One day, while walking around the ponds near her home, she discovered that one of the park benches had gone missing overnight. The idea for *Benched* was born. Cristy lives in White Rock, British Columbia.

orca *currents*

978-1-55469-816-5 $9.95 pb
978-1-55469-817-2 $16.95 lib

Since the death of his father, everyone has been telling Cam that he's the man of the house. Cam takes his responsibility seriously. He keeps the grieving household organized and takes care of his sister. But when the man who had been driving the truck that killed his father seems to be stalking his family, he is not sure he's up for the task. How does the man of the house handle a stalker?

orca *currents*

978-1-55469-807-3 $9.95 pb
978-1-55469-808-0 $16.95 lib

Alone for the first time on the island he calls home, Simon is looking forward to a day of swimming and slacking off. His sister Ellen only wants to make sure they get their chores done. Neither Simon nor Ellen is prepared for the mysterious and potentially dangerous visitor who brings with him an unexpected storm and a riddle that may lead to treasure. Simon and Ellen have to work together to solve the riddle before the stranger—or the weather—destroys their chances.

Titles in the Series

orca currents

orca currents

For more information on all the books
in the Orca Currents series, please visit
www.orcabook.com.